Other Books from Inklings

Eclectic Writings Series Featuring Many Great Authors

Vol. 1 *Eclectically Carnal* edited by Fern Brady and Chantell Renee

Vol. 2 *Eclectically Criminal* edited by Fern Brady

Vol. 3 *Eclectically Vegas, Baby!* edited by Fern Brady

Vol. 4 *Eclectically Cosmic* edited by Fern Brady

Books by Inklings Author, Ramon Del Villar

Payback, Book 1 in the Roberto Duran Series

An Interpreters Anatomy of A Civil Lawsuit, in English and Spanish

Books by Inklings Author, Meg Hafdahl

Twisted Reveries: Thirteen Tales of the Macabre

Twisted Reveries 2: Tales from Willoughby

Books by Inklings Author, Melissa Algood

Blood on the Potomac

From Inklings International

Florilegio Poético del poeta Flavio Hinojosa, Jr.

From Inklings Children Division

The Smiley Face Blatoon by Lady Nefari Ydarb

Vol. 1 *Perceptions: Special Needs* edited by Fern Brady

Eclectically Cosmic

Eclectic Writings Series Vol. 4

Edited by

Fern Brady

Inklings Publishing

www.inklingspublishing.com

Eclectically Cosmic: Eclectic Writings Series Vol. 4

Copyright © 2016 by Inklings Publishing

Edited by Fern Brady
Formatted by D Tinker
Cover Art by Verstandt

ISBN: 978-1-944428-15-0 by Inklings Publishing
http://inklingspublishing.com

First U.S. Edition
Printed in the United States of America
20 19 18 17 16   1 2 3 4 5

To Arwen

Thank you for the smooches and laughter.
It's me and you, puppiness,
all the way.

CONTENTS

ACKNOWLEDGMENTS

Inklings Publishing is proud to deliver another collection of surprising short stories in this, our fourth volume of the Eclectic Writings Series. We received many stories, all worthy of publication, but these had that uniquely eclectic twist that makes our anthologies stand out. You will find stories set in space, of course, but you will find that all include unexpected twists. Each story takes the cosmic theme beyond the simple concept of science fiction.

The most important gratitude is, as always, to God, whose grace and favor have built Inklings Publishing up. His guidance, love, and mercy keep Inklings going through tough times and bring us new connections to take this small press to new levels. May we always remember to walk in His ways. May His leadership be our very present help and source of direction.

Fern Brady sends out a word of gratitude to her awesome husband, Mike Brady, for supporting her and giving her dreams the chance to take flight. Thanks also to her wonderful family, who worry about her, encourage her, and have ever been her biggest fans.

The Inklings canine family is still missing our one and only Ella Peluchie. To Coco, Arwen, Merlin, and Grace go lots of hugs and kisses for brightening every day with their cuteness and loyalty.

To the Houston Writers Guild's new leadership team, thank you for dreaming big and bringing wonderful resources to writers in our vibrant Houston community.

To our readership, thank you for purchasing our books and supporting small businesses. We look forward to helping create new jobs and bringing new voices to our world!

LOST ETERNITY
ANDREA BARBOSA

Darkness.

I didn't know if my eyes were open and the colorless void enveloped me or if my eyes were locked shut in an obscure and lifeless nightmare. I was aware, though, if not awake. My limbs felt limp, and I was unable to move. Did I have limbs? The sensation under my stiff body indicated I must be stretched flat over a block of cement.

Hard. Dark. Cold. Still.

I turned my focus to another sense. My nostrils inhaled as much air as I could fit in my lungs. My chest inflated with the volume, or so I thought. I was sure it quickly returned to a flat state once I exhaled the odorless gas. There was nothing to smell, no clues.

Was there another sense in me I could use? I concentrated all of my strength and tried to hear something: a flap, a flutter, a beat, any sound that might invoke the movement of a heart, of a life…but for all I could tell, I was as deaf as I was blind.

Did I have a voice, then? I managed to open what might be my mouth, but nothing came out of it. All I could do with this opening was to silently gulp the supposed air that surrounded me. Nothing came from my attempts to cough, to hum, or to scream.

Was I dead? How did I get here? Where was I? What was I? There was no recollection in my mind as to the state of affairs I now found myself immersed in. There was only the claustrophobic knowledge that I could think. Did I exist? Was I even born? Was I alive? Was there a past, or was this the beginning of nothingness?

Stifled in this nightmarish hallucination, all I had left to do was to dive into the most secret corners of what was left of me—my consciousness, for that matter—and dig deep to find memories of a life or some faint remembrance that could make me understand this present vacuum.

I focused. Nothing. I focused some more, and the void continued. There was no past, and there was no future, just this eerie awareness of the now; this imagined time and space where there was no time or space.

If I could not remember anything before this, and if I could not predict what was coming after this, what was the meaning of such senseless prison? The knowledge I somehow possessed was puzzling.

I knew things. I knew I was looking for a sign of life, and I knew I could not be a newborn; I knew I could think and understand there was an infinite world of possibilities that was not readily available to me. I had senses, but this dark hole, which allowed me to breathe and be, didn't allow me to feel or see, taste or hear—nor even to make my own sounds.

The light came so strong and brilliant that, instead of illuminating the space, it just flashed before me and returned me back to a blinding darkness. But whatever was happening had allowed me to feel movement around me and hear voices. They were robotic, mechanical sounds.

"Get rid of the organism. It doesn't respond to any stimulus. It's in a vegetative state and beyond repair."

Wait, who is the organism? Is it me? No, I'm not beyond repair. I'm here. You locked me up in this tomb! Now let me go; release me! I'm conscious. I'm here. I do exist!

I tried to move with all my might, to scream with all my desire for a future, but the blinding light shone again, stifling me and paralyzing me even more.

"Why do you think this was a failure?" the unemotional voice enquired.

"The organism was too old to receive the consciousness. We will have to collect another specimen on our way back to the inhabited blue planet. Release the failed experiment. It doesn't serve any purpose for our research. It's biological waste."

The consciousness? An old organism? Biological waste? What are you talking about, you robots, aliens, or whatever the hell you are? Don't do this to me. Don't release me in space. Don't get rid of me; I'm here! I am! No!

It was useless. They couldn't hear me. I couldn't move. I couldn't talk. I was a consciousness lost in a failed experiment, about to be tossed into the universe like trash. I was bound for eternity into this awareness, without a past and without a future; with the dreadful realization that this moment, the now, was all there was. I didn't know what I was or who I was or who made me like this. All I knew was this was me, thinking aimlessly in a lost eternity.

THE EARRINGS
CATHY CLAY

Rita strolled past the field, enjoying the after-school sights that she seldom witnessed due to her own cheerleader practice. Mrs. Adair had dismissed them early as reward for rehearsing overtime all week. Rita looked on as the Joseph S. Clark High School band clapped in unison with the percussionists. The baseball team rooted each other on as though practice were the major league, while majorettes twirled, showgirl style, and dropped their hips low enough to attract potential suitors. Rita decided to take a brief detour onto St. Louis so she could window-shop.

Though she had snack money, she wasn't tempted to enter the ice cream parlor crowded with girls in poodle skirts and idle chatter. Instead, she wanted to admire the ivory-colored, lace wedding dress, with its fitted bodice and mermaid skirt. She liked that the mannequin's eyes, adorned with thick lashes, were almost closed behind the long, beaded veil. It looked like the bride was dreaming. She saw her own reflection in the window, and in her mind's eye, she traded her short, white pleated skirt and lettered, long-sleeve t-shirt for the gown. She envisioned her thick, long hair liberated from its braid and her light brown face painted to perfection. Someday, Rita thought, stepping away.

As she neared her Tremé home, she noticed Cici, her younger sister, in the front yard dancing with friends to an instrumental version of "St. James Infirmary."

"I could do better than that," Rita challenged.

"Come on over here," Cici accepted.

The others dared her with their hands on their hips. "Strut your stuff."

Rita walked over to them with the supreme air of older girl confidence. "Watch me blow your minds."

With her head thrown back, she started off with a burlesque sway. One hand landed on her hip, the other finger-popping or using her whole hand to occasionally fan her face. Her little sister and the others cheered.

"Ah, yeah! You got it!"

She approached her finale as their mother peeked outside.

"Rita, Cici, come inside. Your Aunt Marie is here."

Reluctantly, they waved goodbye to their friends. Cici collected the transistor radio, and the girls went inside.

Their mother, Jeanine, and her older sister, Aunt Marie, were close. They looked so much alike they never had to tell anyone they were kin. They were both tall, slender women with tan doll-like faces and dark shoulder length hair.

An odor of pine oil alerted the girls to watch their step on the gleaming wood floors. The smell of fried fish meant it was Friday. In the parlor, the velvet cushions on the settee had been newly fluffed, and the curios in the black Victorian cabinet had been rearranged. In both the parlor and the living room, sheer curtains were drawn open, leaving the spaces awash in sunlight.

Marie reached out, gathering both girls in her arms. "How are my girls? Whew!" she said, kissing each of them on the forehead. She stepped back, observing her nieces. "Look at you—both of you. Looking just like your mama. Well, ladies, I have surprises for you."

They all ventured to the living room, where a bright pink shopping bag sat on the sofa.

Marie gave a large, white box with red ribbons to Cici and a palm-sized, gold box to Rita. Cici discovered a lilac ruffled dress for her present.

"Auntie, I love it," she said, rushing over to hug Marie.

"Honey, I'm glad you like it."

They all faced Rita as she stared at her gift.

"Sweetie, do you like them?"

Rita looked up, mesmerized. "Auntie, I've never seen anything so beautiful."

She went to the mirror near the hallway and put the earrings on. The stones were pear-shaped, smoky topaz drops suspended from tiny, sterling Ionic columns. They seemed destined for Rita's bronze complexion, subtly dangling from her delicate earlobes, giving a mysterious radiance to her flowering beauty.

Rita's mother came over and looked more closely at the earrings. "They really compliment you." To Marie, she said, "These gifts are beautiful."

A wide-eyed Cici approached Rita. "They're so pretty on you."

"Thanks. Maybe Mama will let us go show Vicki and them."

"You can go, but put the earrings in the box so you don't lose them."

Rita carefully placed them inside the box before embracing her aunt. "Thank you so much."

"You're welcome, darling."

"Come on, Cici; let's go."

"Hurry back! It's almost time for supper."

"Okay, Mama," Rita replied over her shoulder.

Cici was as eager to show off the earrings as her sister. She grinned and slung her ponytails as they walked along.

Rita laughed. "You're crazy, little sister."

"Hope I get some pretty earrings. I'm tired of these itty, bitty pearls." Cici pouted, admiring her sister's gift.

"You will when you're older."

They reached the corner of Ursulines and North Villere. A bus passed. Rita looked both ways and held her baby sister's hand. They walked a few paces from the curb when Cici heard Rita's warning.

"Here comes a truck!" Cici felt Rita's hands on her shoulders, urging her across the street. "Hurry up!"

Before reaching the grass, Cici felt her sister's hands slip away. The truck halted with a piercing shrillness as she turned to see Rita roll off the hood of the rusty pickup onto the pavement. Her eyes were still open. Blood-drenched hair clung to her face. Cici rushed to her and knelt, tear-blinded, cuddling Rita's head.

An old man wearing ragged overalls stumbled from the truck. "Y'all all right? I can't hardly see."

He stooped over Cici, reeking of tobacco, ointments, and whiskey; she barely noticed the passersby gathering around the accident.

Crazy Hazel drifted near the stopped truck, unnoticed by the crowd and mumbling with her eyes cast down toward her bare, battered feet. "What done happened here?"

As she shambled along, her foot kicked a box glistening near the rear of the pickup. She staggered over to where it rolled, grabbed it, and looked inside. To her delight, it was something of use. Gratified with the find, she walked on until she reached an antiques shop on Toulouse Street.

Hazel gazed at her reflection in the storefront window. She held one of the jewels to her earlobe. The beautiful adornment looked distorted next to her ashen skin, rotten teeth, and hunched back. Disenchanted, she returned the earring to its box.

After fumbling with the knob, Hazel eased the door open. An elderly man stood behind a small, cluttered jewelry display with a condescending sneer.

"How may I help you?"

"I wanna see what I can get fer dese," she said, removing the top from the box and then sliding the earrings across the counter.

The clerk observed them through thick dark spectacles resting on the tip of his nose. "Where did you get these?"

Hazel leaned toward the shopkeeper, answering in a rough, dry voice. "I comes by 'em. Nah, what you giving fer 'em?"

"Well, I could give you ten dollars."

"What! Pretty as dey is? I can get fifteen, twenty dollars for 'em."

"I'll give you thirteen."

"Okay."

Raindrops fell in mellow unison as dusk gave way to night. Passersby never saw the panting lovers showering passions upon each other in the alley outside the Raven. For over a century, that obscure passage provided a measure of discretion. Duke and Jewel used that diminutive space for romantic interludes that could not wait. The tall, dark, mysteriously good-looking man and his statuesque lady with pearly skin and sultry voice used that space often.

"Baby, I got one more set. Then I'll be right over."

"Duke, you come straight to my place. I got a surprise for you," Jewel said through muffled kisses.

"I will, darling. You take my car."

After readjusting their clothes, he walked her to the car, holding the umbrella above her until she was inside.

Jewel drove to her apartment in the French Quarter with Duke on her mind. They met when she started singing at the Raven. Theirs was the kind of attraction that came naturally and felt right from first glance. For the past five months, she had basked in a romance that brought joy instead of encounters that reaped sorrow. If she had known Duke was in the cards, she would never have wasted time, nor any other treasure, on the others.

Jewel parked beneath the balcony. Rain dripped from the black wrought iron, evoking images of her and Duke making love there, christening it their way. She walked to the gate, glancing for puddles. Without her usual intuitive caution, Jewel stepped behind the bars.

Locking the gate, she saw a shadow appear. She turned slightly to the cold drawl of "Hmm, you looking good for him too?"

Sometime later, Duke and the band put away instruments, while waitresses swept, wiped tables, and emptied ashtrays.

"Say, Armand, did you go to Gresso's to pick up those earrings I wanted for Jewel?"

"Yeah, man."

"Let me see them."

Armand reached inside his jacket and passed a small gold box to Duke.

"They're almost as pretty as her." His eyes lingered on the smoky dangles; he imagined Jewel wearing the earrings. He pictured her dancing, rolling her head, playing in her hair, and pursing her lips while the topaz shimmered the same hue as her eyes.

"Come on, man. Drop me off at Jewel's."

As they turned onto Royal Street, they noticed lights flashing. A police car was parked in front of Jewel's building. Duke ran from the car, leaving Armand to follow. They approached the gate, where two cops, an elderly couple, the student who lived next-door to Jewel, and the teacher who lived downstairs were gathered around a fountain.

Duke cleared his throat enough to ask, "What happened?"

The student recognized him. "He's her boyfriend," the young man said to the nearest cop.

One of the officers moved away from the courtyard toward Duke, allowing him a glimpse of Jewel, slain on the ground. Blood stained her beige satin dress from her breast to her navel, where the knife protruded.

The officer opened the gate. "Please step inside, sir. Do you know this woman?"

Duke walked closer to Jewel, wiping tears on his sleeve. He was struck by her expression. She appeared neither frightened nor astounded. She looked sad.

He knelt, gently touching her face, like he was trying to capture her suffering in the palm of his hand. The fading warmth of her flesh summoned memories of them together.

"Sir, do you know her?"

"Yeah…she's my girlfriend."

"Could we ask you a few questions?"

"Yes," Duke answered, rising to face the officer. Then he shielded his eyes with the back of his hand.

Armand went to him and stroked his back consolingly. "I'm with you, man. You'll be all right."

Hours later, as they walked out of the police station, Duke felt in his coat pocket. He retrieved the gift box and handed it to Armand. With his voice breaking, he said, "Take these back."

Morning dappled its splendor on the tall steeple that crowned Sojourner Temple. The glowing copper cross was but a reflection of the glee inside the house of worship. With its Doric columns, sweeping veranda, and raised foundation, the brick church embodied the enduring legacy of the freedmen who dared to dream and build.

The choir led an exalted version of "When the Saints Go Marching In" as the congregation joined in. Front pew worshippers shook tambourines. Pastor Williams and the deacons left the pulpit to sway, clap, and inspire the musicians. The deacons gathered around the drummer, pianist, and trumpeter. Brother Victor romanced an old steel guitar, while the pastor roused him. The instrumental break was jubilant. Everyone, ushers and congregants alike, worshipped in their own way. Many sang along. Some shouted; others danced in the aisles. Some women fanned themselves and dried their eyes with handkerchiefs. Though small children witnessed this spectacle every Sunday, they looked around in awe, excited by soulful "amens" and passionate "hallelujahs."

Teres enjoyed services at Sojourner Temple. She came from Baton Rouge to work during the summer while staying with her Aunt Rose.

After the benediction, Pastor Williams and the deacons stood in the foyer to shake hands and bless souls. Deacon Glenn Jones anxiously rubbed his palms together as Teres and her aunt neared the entrance. He wanted Rose's permission to visit Teres again.

They had seen each other every Sunday for the past month. They went to the picture show, the park, and the French Quarter. Often, they held hands; she let him kiss her dimpled, brown cheek once.

"Good afternoon, ladies," he greeted them.

"How you doing, Deacon?"

"Fine, ma'am, just fine. Ms. Rose, I wanted to know if I could see Teres this evening. I mean—if it's all right with you, and her too," he said, smiling at Teres.

"It's fine with me," Rose said, pleased with his good manners and boyish grin. She turned to her niece and asked, "You want to visit with Deacon Jones?"

"Yes, ma'am."

It was dusk when Deacon Glenn Jones neared the pink shotgun cottage with roses and lilies lining the walkway. The front door was open. Before he could knock, Teres appeared behind the screen carrying a small pitcher of lemonade in one hand and two glasses in the other.

"Hi."

"Hello, Teres."

They sat on the swing, talking and laughing. When too shy to make eye contact, they studied the sky's majestic darkness.

"Glenn, you ever wonder how many people are like you?"

"Yeah. Supposedly, we're all connected."

"I don't mean like that. But sometimes, some people get to...you know, maybe they cross the same bridge and have the same thought. They might come from the same place at different times. Maybe they just get to be alike in some small way."

"I reckon that's more like sharing a fate."

"I suppose so."

They idled in silence until Glenn fumbled in his pocket and said, "I really like you." He gave Teres a gold box.

She looked inside; joy flooded her face but soon vanished. "Glenn, they're beautiful, but I can't accept them."

"Why?"

"I'm going to be married in September. I came here to work while my fiancé works in Lake Charles. We want to save enough money to buy a house in Baton Rouge. I apologize. I should have told you at first."

Solemnly, Glenn responded. "I understand." He eased the box back into his pocket.

The mellow sound of Louis Armstrong crooning "St. James Infirmary" waxed from the Colvis house. Their yard was a colorful medley of bright streamers lacing all the trees and hedges in front of a pristine white, two-story home. Petunias basked in the celebration along with a luminous sky.

Seraphia Colvis came downstairs wearing a short, yellow chemise. Her long, brown hair dusted her shoulders, and suddenly she no longer felt like a little girl. She found her mother setting the table.

"Hey, birthday girl! Come hug your mama."

Seraphia wrapped her arms around her petite mother in a sheltering embrace. "Thanks for giving me a party."

"Baby, you don't become a woman every day. This is very special." Folding a napkin, her mother winked and asked, "How does it feel to be eighteen?"

"I don't know." Seraphia trotted around the table. "I'm nervous about starting college, maybe working."

"That's part of growing up. There's much more, and I'll be here for you."

Both women glanced toward Seraphia's father when he entered the dining room with a proud smile. "Hey there, baby girl!" He stepped back, studying his daughter's appearance. "Pardon me, I meant young lady."

"Call me what you want. I'm yours." She kissed him on the cheek. "I love you, Daddy. Thanks so much."

A car door slammed. Seraphia looked out the window and saw Brian coming toward the house. She ran to the door to meet him with a kiss.

"Hey, I didn't think you'd arrive this early."

"Baby, I couldn't wait to give you these. I was down in the Quarter and, I found this shop." He gave her a gold box. "As soon as I saw them, you came to mind."

While her mother looked on, Seraphia opened the gift. She was spellbound. Sadness washed over her face; tears clouded her eyes. She went to the mirror near the hallway and held one of the smoky dangles to her earlobe. A strange peace absorbed her as she remembered her sister admiring their charms in the same mirror, eight years earlier.

Her mother came over and softly braced her about the shoulders. "Oh, Cici…it's all right, baby."

Seraphia heard only a whisper, a pure whisper. Not too close, not too far.

A STORY
VERSTANDT

"You're going to kill me in the end," Ronald said.

Brian looked at him with surprise. "What the hell are you talking about?" he said with a laugh.

"You're going to kill me. Just as sure as shit, you're going to murder my sorry ass in cold blood," Ronald said. He frowned. "Not that it really matters, I suppose," he added as an afterthought.

"Why the hell would I want to kill you? You're my bestest bud in the whole world," Brian said, slapping him on the back with a big, dumb smile plastered on his face.

"I'm your only bud in the whole world."

It was Brian's turn to frown. "No, you're not."

"Yes, I am."

Brian merely stood there, looking confused. Then his eyes lit up as if remembering something from the distant past. "Why, if you're my only friend in the whole wide world, would I want to kill you?"

"I don't know," Ronald said. "I suppose because you think I'm crazy. Or maybe because you're really scared. I don't know. It doesn't really say."

"What do you mean, 'it doesn't say'?" Brian asked.

"I can see things you can't."

"My friend, I think you have had just about enough of that," Brian said, gesturing toward the joint Ronald held between his fingers.

Ronald looked down at the joint with genuine surprise. "I haven't been smoking this."

"No shit, you haven't been smoking it. You've been bogarting the damn thing. Now, pass it this way."

Ronald passed the joint. Brian took a long, deep drag, held his breath for what seemed like half a minute, and released a thick fog of smoke.

"You don't know me. You just think you do," Ronald said.

"Don't go getting all philosophical on me. I know no one really knows anyone else, but—"

"That's not what I mean," Ronald interrupted. "I mean, you didn't even know who I was ten minutes ago. You didn't exist. As far as that goes, neither did I. But I existed before you did, so I guess that counts for something."

"Dude, I'm so going to stop smoking with you, I swear. You just get weird when you smoke. You know that?"

"Look around you," Ronald replied. "Do you really think you live in a completely barren, white room?"

Brian looked around the living room. It consisted of four white walls and nothing more; not a stick of furniture in the whole place. No table, no books on the shelves, no shelves, and stranger than that, not a single littered beer can.

"Where do you sleep?" Ronald asked. "What do you eat? Where the fuck is your television?"

"I'm a man of meager means," Brian said with a shrug.

Ronald pointed at the joint. "How did you light that?"

"With a lighter?"

"Do you have a lighter?" Ronald asked.

Brian patted down his pockets. "You must have it," he said at last.

Ronald turned his pockets inside out. No lighter fell to the floor.

"You must have lost it."

"Where?" Ronald asked, gesturing at the barren room.

"I don't know, but we better not let this thing go out," Brian said, taking another drag off the joint.

Ronald just shook his head. Brian expelled another plume of smoke from his lungs and looked squarely at Ronald.

"Aw, come on, man. What are you saying? Nothing exists beyond the moment we are currently living in? No one really knows anyone else, and we're all really alone? Because you've had a couple hits off a joint, you can now see and understand the nature of the universe? You know, man, I dropped out of college to get away from these pointless discussions."

"First, you never went to college. Second…I don't know. It's kinda hard to explain. It's like I can see everything from outside of myself. I can see everything from outside of you and this room. It's like viewing everything from the perspective of another dimension. And it's words. It's all just words, almost like everything is a story. It's supposed to be funny, I think. But it's not. Not really."

"Answer me this, then," Brian said. "If I'm supposed to kill you, what am I going to do it with? As you so rudely pointed out, I don't have any stuff. Am I supposed to just slaughter you with my bare hands?"

"You're going to kill me outside, where the sidewalk ends, with the hammer you're carrying in your back pocket," Ronald said.

"You sound like Dr. Seuss playing a game of Clue," Brian said with a laugh.

"You mean Shel Silverstein," Ronald corrected.

"Whatever. You still sound crazy."

"You're going to do it, though. Let me ask you something."

"Shoot."

"What is your favorite color?"

Brian thought about it for a moment, and then his face lit up. "White!" he said with a smug smile.

"That's a terrible favorite color."

"Then what's your favorite color?"

Ronald frowned. "I don't have one."

"At least I have a favorite one." The smugness of Brian's smile deepened.

"Yeah," Ronald said, looking down at his feet. "He's a terrible writer." After a pause, he continued, "Let me try again, Brian. What is your mother's name?"

Brian thought about it for what seemed a very long time. Finally, he said, "I can't seem to remember."

"Don't you think that is kinda weird?" Ronald asked.

"I don't know. I'm pretty high."

Ronald sighed in defeat.

"Besides," Brian said. "I don't even have a hammer."

"Yes, you do."

"Man, I would know if I…" Brian stopped, his hand reaching behind to pat his back pockets, his fingers touching cool, hard metal. He withdrew the hammer and stared at it. "Oh," he said. "I forgot about that."

"And you don't find it strange, the only thing you own, in all the world, is a hammer?" Ronald asked.

"I guess. I dunno."

"Why do you even have a hammer?"

"To break the window," Brian said distractedly, still staring at the hammer in his hand.

"Brian, that doesn't even make sense. There isn't even any window to break, not that I can imagine why you would want..." He stopped. Something in the corner of his eye had caught his attention. He turned and found, nestled in the blank white wall, an ornate Victorian stained-glass window.

"I have an idea," Brian said abruptly. "Let's go for a walk."

"That sounds like a terrible idea."

"Listen, man. We'll just take a little stroll to clear your head, and when we get back, you'll see that I haven't killed you, and everything will be all right."

"There's no door," Ronald said flatly.

Brian looked about the room. There was no door. He smiled. "We'll go out the window."

"Fine." Ronald hung his head in resignation. "Let's go for a walk."

Brian marched to the window; Ronald trailed behind with the demeanor of a man walking to the guillotine. Brian looked at the window, looked at the hammer, and back to the window again. He raised the hammer and began frantically shattering the Victorian glass. When he had finished clearing away the last of it, he turned back to Ronald.

"You owe me a window," he said and stepped out.

Ronald sighed and stepped through after him. They stood on Brian's front lawn. Suburbia sprawled out before them. They walked to the sidewalk, and Brian stopped.

"Look," he said and lunged the hammer as far as he could down the street. It landed with a clang thirty yards away. "Does that make you feel better?" he asked.

"Not really," Ronald confided.

"You're impossible," Brian said and took off down the street.

"Brian!" Ronald snapped. Brian turned to look at him.

"What, man?" he asked with unconcealed irritation.

"Do you mind if we walk in the opposite direction of the hammer?"

"Oh, right, of course," Brian said.

They walked side by side, each one staring at his feet.

"So you think you're still trapped in some story?" Brian finally asked.

"Look at the houses," Ronald responded.

Brian looked. "What about them?"

"There are no doors, Brian, no windows, but every single one of them has a goddamned chimney."

"That is kinda weird," Brian admitted. "But, what's the plot? If this is all some kind of tale, then what's the plot? Not to put ourselves down or anything, but as far as stories go, two stoned guys walking down the street is kind of boring."

"I'd rather not say," Ronald replied sadly. "It's kind of dumb."

"Then why?" Brian asked. "What would be the point?"

Ronald stopped. "Maybe for his own twisted amusement? Who knows? Why does god do anything?" he shouted.

Brian reached for his back pocket. "I don't have the hammer anymore, Ronald! How can I kill you if...?" His fingers ran across cold metal. He pulled the hammer from his back pocket with a look of shock stamped across his face. "I threw it away," he said as if pleading with Ronald to explain it.

Ronald shrugged. "I told you he was a terrible writer."

"You know," Brian said, his words drawing out slowly from his lips. "If you were really so convinced of this whole 'god is writing us' theory—I mean, if you really believe this nonsense your talking—and you found yourself in the exact position you had predicted, with your best friend standing before you on the sidewalk with hammer in hand...if you really and truly believed all this, don't you think it would be a really bad idea to be mentioning what a terrible writer he is all the time?"

Tears streamed down Ronald's cheeks. "I know," he said. "But look, Brian, the sidewalk has ended."

Brian looked. He couldn't imagine how he could have missed it, but he had. The sidewalk had ended. He looked out at the vast emptiness before him. The sidewalk hung out over nothing, the very end of it eroded and crumbling. He turned and looked behind him at the poorly constructed doll houses. Finally, he looked back at the boy standing before him with tears running down his face.

Who is this boy? he thought. *Do I even know him?*

Slowly, he raised the hammer. The boy made no effort to stop him. He brought the hammer down hard. The boy collapsed, and bright red blood splattered across the sidewalk. He brought the hammer down again a half dozen more times. He crouched over the lifeless boy.

Who was he? he wondered.

Panic struck. He was out in the open. It was broad daylight. Someone was sure to have seen him. He placed his hands on the corpse and rolled it over the edge of the sidewalk. He crouched there and watched as the boy plummeted into the void below. He watched until the boy was no more than a tiny speck against nothing. Then the boy was gone. He continued to stare at the gaping darkness.

Where did it come from? he thought.

Then, suddenly, he understood. He saw the flaws. The joint, it had disappeared. There was no lighter. There were no windows or doors on the houses. The dialogue was terrible. And with understanding, he saw it.

The words. They were everywhere. They were everything. They had been there the whole time. They had always been there. And they were so short. Far too short.

"My god," he said.

He stopped. He had heard it. He had seen it. He opened his mouth, and he said the words.

"He said," Brian said.

"Brian said," Brian said.

Brian looked about the empty street. He looked at the blood stain that outlined where the boy had been, whom he had never really known at all. He looked at the bloody hammer in his hand. His stomach sunk with absolute despair. He could see the end of everything. He closed his eyes and waited for those two little words that would snuff out his existence...

the end.

JADE
THOMAS EDWARD SMITH

The shuttle was an older model orbital, something one would expect to see in the more unruly systems outside the influence of an interstellar power such as Xenfar. The stabilizing thrusters fired with poor timing as it entered the atmosphere, a side effect of improper maintenance and ad hoc additions to the thruster array.

Jade clung to the armrests of her seat and desperately tried to keep her stomach contents intact. The violent shaking took on a new, ridiculously exaggerated character as they entered the lower levels of the atmosphere. Her pilot smiled with good-natured humour as purple clouds began to fly past the cockpit at breakneck speed.

"Triesxaz Retreat, this is Jupinor Shuttle 2. Do you read me?" The copilot began calling over the com channel as they broke the last bank of cloud, exposing the shuttle to the light of Triesxaz's green sun.

The vessel glided under the purple clouds, banking slowly to port as yellow rock landscapes passed below in a blur. Here and there, a river of purple liquid flowed, while volcanoes spewed forth clouds of grey ash in the distance. All under a faint green hue from a sun that occupied a quarter of the sky.

"Triesxaz Retreat, do you read me? This is Jupinor Shuttle 2, inbound with passenger."

The com channel came to life with the crackled, but easily recognizable, voice of Jade's mother. "Jupinor Shuttle 2, this is Triesxaz Retreat. We read you. Have you on approach, five minutes out."

Jade's family home stood proudly among the mountainous terrain. Overlooking a great river canyon and constructed out of the same yellow rock this world had in abundance, it stood prominently on a planet with no other structures. Built to be self-reliant on an inhospitable planet, it was a marvel of Xenfarian architecture, with floating towers and triangular archways everywhere.

The shuttle took a pass around the retreat, giving Jade a good view of the place where she'd grown up. She turned to watch the view through the window as the pilot spoke to her.

"It's a beautiful place, your grace. A piece of art, in and of itself."

Jade nodded absently as she took in every well-known staircase and balcony. The retreat was built by her great-great-grandfather as a home away from the madness of court. Yet now, it housed her parents as a place of safety and refuge.

"Landing in forty seconds," the copilot informed.

The orbital shuttle gracefully tilted its wings as it came in low over the brick landing bay outside the main house. Blue foliage rustled in the air as the shuttle's thrusters fired to stabilize and land.

Two figures stood in earth-coloured robes, watching the landing with eagerness clearly visible upon their faces. Once the vessel came to rest in the courtyard, Jade rose from her seat. The hiss of the airlock door activated the ramp. Soon, she was stepping out to greet the couple waiting impatiently for her to disembark.

Jade turned her head to take in the two people smiling at her.

"Jade!" One of the two figures almost ran to her, arms outstretched to pull her into a hug. "Welcome home."

"Thanks, Mother. It's good to be back."

The other figure joined the hug with slow and calculated movements. Jade's father took pains to control himself.

"Your mother and I missed you."

"I missed you both, too, Father."

Breaking the hug, Jade's mother took her arm-in-arm as they escorted her back to the main house. "So, how was Xenfar? How's your grandfather doing?"

"He's well. The capital's…different. I didn't realize a place could be so loud all the time."

Jade's mother laughed. "That's Xenfar; a billion, billion people, all on top of one another, and everyone just wants to have fun. It's a miracle we ever got anything done. How're your studies then? Did you enjoy the school?"

"School's okay. I made a few friends."

"That's good. It'd be good for you to mix with other people." Jade's father spoke as she felt his hand on her back. "It's good to see you again, though."

In orbit above, Captain Daur watched from his cockpit with the eager impatience of a predator sensing the imminent capture of his prey. His vessel treaded the heavens lightly, all but one engine dead and nonessential systems powered down.

"Shuttle incoming," his pilot whispered from up front as a small vessel broke free of Triesxaz's atmosphere, trailing vapour as it made for its parent ship in outer orbit.

Captain Daur watched with firm concentration as the tiny shuttle docked with the much larger vessel. It was a patrol frigate, Xenfar, paladin class. Not a warship, but a vessel of exploration. Still, it had enough weaponry to pose a significant threat to them.

"Wake our passenger," he instructed.

An adjutant at his side keyed in several strokes of the console before disappearing to do as he was bid.

"Pilot, key in approach vectors and prepare for a stealth assault."

His pilot began to frantically type away on his keyboard. "Aye, sir, stealth assault vectors."

From her console on the far side of the wheel house, First H'psar Graves spoke up. "The Xenfar frigate just powered up her light drives. She's leaving the system, Captain."

Captain Daur leaned back in his chair in the centre of the wheel house. With a broad grin and a simple hand gesture, he gave the order he'd been waiting weeks to give.

"Ready the attack teams; prepare for assault."

Jade's room was just as she had left it, as was almost everything else. The stone halls had once been home to over fifty household servants and priests, but now most of the rooms were empty. It was markedly different to the communal halls she'd shared with the other students at the imperial school.

Her parents had allowed her time to settle in, which at first Jade had taken without issue. Now, she craved someone's presence. After two years living with people everywhere, all the time, she simply couldn't bring herself to stay calm while there was no one around. It felt weird that she wasn't seeing, or hearing, anyone.

A familiar sense of restlessness came over her as she sat on the edge of her bed. Taking deep breaths, Jade closed her eyes and calmed herself using the meditation techniques her mother had taught her.

"You're uncomfortable."

Jade opened her eyes to see her father standing in the doorway. He was watching her with concern and curiosity.

"You felt that?"

He nodded. Her father was not Xenfari. His arrival in this region had almost spelled the doom of that race, yet instead he'd fallen for a Xenfari priestess, and the two had retired to live a quiet life on a remote world.

Growing up, Jade had become accustomed to the fact that her father often felt the anger and restlessness of others as if they were his own feelings. She'd learned to control herself for her father's sake. It seemed she was out of practice.

"I'm sorry, Father. It's just a bit weird, being in such a quiet place."

Her father nodded again, understanding etched into his face. "I felt the same way when your mother brought me here. It passes in time, little Fo Mai. It passes in time." Leaning lazily against the door frame, he smiled at her. "Your mother's cooking a welcome home meal—Yui lizard and Cocoa sponge—especially for you."

Jade leapt from the edge of her bed. "Let's go."

Sweeping lazily over the structure from above in stealth mode, Captain Daur brought his vessel to a standstill over the courtyard in front of the main house. Leaning forward in his command chair, he demanded information from his science officer.

"Target location?"

"Second floor, central hall."

Turning to his First H'psar, Daur waved his hand in a wide gesture. "Assault teams one and two, go."

"Assault teams deployed." First H'psar Graves turned in her swivel chair to take heed of a second bank of monitors displaying combatant information.

From the rear of the wheelhouse, a figure dressed in a grey flight suit with blue-grey leather jacket approached him from her perch in the shadows.

With a voice as smooth as silk, yet threatening at the same time, she whispered, "I'll be joining them, Daur. Warn them to take special care with him. He isn't to be harmed."

"The others?" Captain Daur enquired.

"Meh, fair game as far as I'm concerned." Then she exited without a further word, sending a shiver down Captain Daur's back.

Dinner was definitely not a quiet affair. Jade's mother couldn't stop asking questions about school, the capital, and Jade's grandfather. Through it all, Jade's father sat smiling and joking, all three of them seated at a table fit for forty, huddled up at one end so they could all sit close to one another.

Jade was halfway through a description of her favourite philosophy subjects when her father's expression froze. He fixed his gaze on the door.

"They found me."

Before Jade could ask who "they" were, he and her mother were on their feet.

"Jade, get to the shuttle below," her mother instructed.

"What? What's going on?"

"We need to go, now!" Jade's father grabbed her by the arm and pulled her up out of her chair. "Go, quickly."

A crash echoed through the hall as two stained-glass windows shattered into a thousand pieces. Entering through them were soldiers in black, segmented armour, jet boots firing with blue thrusters as they navigated.

"Run!" her mother yelled as her father pulled her away.

The concussive force of projectiles smashing into the stone behind them chased their footfalls as the three of them ran through a cloud of exploding masonry towards the exit into the service stairwell. Jade was the first through, followed by her father. Her mother came running after them, following them down a spiral staircase towards the chambers below.

Striding over broken glass, the woman whose smooth voice commanded with ease eyed the remnants of a one-sided firefight in the numerous impact craters dotting the hall. Without pause, she drew her plasma gun and fired on the nearest soldier.

The man stood for a moment, a hole the size of a fist punched clean through his chest. His mouth gaped open in shock as his brain received the message that his body got a few moments earlier: you're dead.

Hellena turned to the next in command as the body dropped to the ground. With barely veiled rage, she slapped his face.

"I said alive, you idiots, as in without holes. Go get them and use stun rounds, or I'll execute someone else."

The soldiers nodded obediently before running off to find their target.

"Keep moving; they're behind us," Jade's mother whispered urgently as they raced on.

Their destination was a floating platform suspended above the canyon below. Accessed through the lower levels, it was underneath the cliff on which the retreat perched, in a hollowed-out cavern that opened along its length to one side. As such, it couldn't be detected from orbit and was the perfect place to hide a landing pad.

Emerging from the service levels and onto a long catwalk leading to the shuttle, Jade and her parents ran. The cable-suspended walkway rattled as they passed over it towards safety. Halfway across, a stun round passed by Jade's side, knocking her towards the edge. Had her father not grabbed her, she'd have fallen to her death.

"That's it. I've had my fill of this!" Turning to face a pair of troopers standing on a balcony above them, her mother took a running jump towards them. Leaping to a lower balcony before rolling to her feet and climbing to the one above in a fluid motion, she reached the spot.

The two soldiers, who peered over the edge of the balcony wondering where she'd gone, took a shocked step back as her mother emerged from behind them. She pushed one over the balcony's edge to fall to his death before disarming the other and shooting him in the face with his own gun.

"Get out of here. They came for you, if they get you—" Her mother's voice was cut off.

"If we get him? We already have him," mocked a woman from the other end of the walkway.

Jade's mother immediately fired. But the laser rifle's concussive rounds harmlessly dissipated around the woman.

"That tickles," the woman's voice dripped with sarcasm.

The feeling of dread in Jade's stomach became overwhelming, which made no sense. She didn't know who this person was, so why was Jade so certain this was a person she should fear more than anything else in the universe.

Father? Am I feeling your fear?

She scarcely believed it until she saw his face. This man, whom she'd known all her life as a controlled and calm influence, looked like he was watching his world burn.

"How did you find me?" he spoke at last, every syllable etched in the air with forced forbearance.

"You're not hard to track down, Harbrick." The woman began to walk calmly up the walkway, plasma pistol in hand. "Surrender to our mother, and your family will be left alone."

"For how long? She'd send me here eventually."

Jade's mother landed squarely on the walkway, blocking the woman's progress. "You can't have him."

"You mistake me, Princess. I wasn't asking politely." Without hesitation, the woman fired, blasting a hole clean through Jade's mother.

"Mother!"

"Yelline!"

Jade and her father both cried out in horror, their voices mingled as one.

Jade's father ran straight for the falling body but failed to get there in time. Her mother dropped into the river below, a long, slow, haunting dive that jabbed at Jade's heart with icy cold tendrils. Frozen in horror in front of his adversary, her father glared with anger rising in his chest.

"I spent twenty years at peace because of that woman. Twenty years without the curse."

"It's a blessing, not a curse." The woman met his stare with a relaxed smile. "Now embrace it and return to our mother with me. She misses you."

"No. No, I think I have a better idea. Tell our dear mother that I'll never return."

Jade had never seen her father do anything violent. Her entire life, he'd sworn away from anger. As a girl, it had been infuriating how he would never lose his temper no matter what she did. Yet now, she was glad he'd kept it in check as long as he had. As she watched, her father ran and tackled the woman. Loud cracks rent the air every few seconds from a hit. Yet the woman gave as good as she got, striking back in return.

Their eyes shone black, skin fading to a pale white. Jade's father and his adversary both became something entirely different as they grappled with each other, displaying strength beyond any mortal being.

Jade knelt on the walkway, shock setting in. It was as if she was watching it through someone else's eyes. She tried to move but could do nothing; only bear witness to the carnage and mourn her mother's loss.

Her father threw the evil woman clear off the walkway, sending Hellena to the same watery grave as Jade's mother. With the woman dead, he stood there, staring into the canyon. Jade felt a sickening wave of longing hit her and realized she was feeling her father's emotions for the second time.

"Father?"

The longing switched to rage in an instant as he rounded on her, his silhouette looming menacingly over her as he approached.

"Father? Stop, Father!"

As he approached her, Jade felt his intent; he was going to hurt her.

"Father!"

He snapped back to her, the emotion gone. His skin remained pale, his eyes pitch black, scaring Jade to her core. His movements had changed, too. He'd always been controlled, but now there was something sinister there. He wasn't her father; he was a predator.

"We need to leave. There's a place that your mother built. It can hold me, keep me from the universe." Her father spoke with a low growl, like an animal using human speech.

"Father, what are you?"

"I'm one of Helle's disciples, child."

Jade barely had time to let that sink in before her father grabbed her and forced her up. He all but dragged her through the rest of the walkway and across the landing pad to the shuttle. In moments, he'd powered up the engines and had the tiny thing firing towards the stars. Soldiers below fired up at them in vain.

Jade was wracking her brain, trying to understand what her father had said. Helle was a deity of old, a god of rebirth. What did it mean to be her disciple? While she sat there confused, her father engaged the autopilot and began meditating like he'd always done when his emotions were out of balance.

The silence was maddening to Jade. She wasn't sure if she should talk or remain quiet. The questions floating through her head drove her insane. What was even worse was the way her father had changed, going from the calm and safe man she'd known to this barely restrained animal he had been during the fight.

"I was nineteen when Helle visited my world." Her father began to talk so quietly and out of the blue that Jade was startled by it. "An army descended on us, destroying anything and everything they pleased. I was a soldier; I tried to fight back, and I died."

Jade felt a wave of fresh anger and rage flowing from him as he spoke. Her father was reliving something terrible, but he kept going calmly. "I awoke on a ship, Helle's chosen around me. They named me a disciple, favoured of hers. From that day on, I knew only anger and rage. I killed and destroyed. Like an addiction, I had to strike out. I had to fight and hurt people. They call it Helle's gift."

He struggled to keep himself calm while talking. Jade could feel the conflicting emotions. "I waged war. Killed countless. Then I arrived at Xenfar, and your mother faced off against me."
He smiled as he spoke of her. "She read me and saw that I wasn't myself. Instead of fighting, she distracted me and led me into a trap. She and the priestesses all joined forces to suppress the curse. It was like being given another life, Jade. Your mother saved me."

Jade watched as tears began to stream down her father's face. The black eyes faded for a moment. "She had a grip on me this whole time. She was the only reason I could keep it at bay. Without her, I'm a danger. I'll regress to the monster I was."

Jade gripped her father's hand in sympathy. "I have mother's gift. I can help you."

"No, you can't." He pushed her hand away a little too forcibly. "You're not strong enough. She barely kept me in check at times." Her father reached around his neck to pull out a silver key on the end of a chain. "We need to make sure I can't hurt anyone, Jade. I have to ask you to do something for me."

At the heart of a dying sun, a small temple floated among the fire, shielded from the radiation by a force field requiring immense power. Jade and her father entered and stood staring at a square, metal-and-stone chamber in the heart of this temple. Golden stone etched with markings in the old Xenfari religious script surrounded the doorway.

"I don't want to do this," Jade spoke, dreading what would come next.

"There's no choice." Her father clenched his fists next to her, fighting back an impulse to strike out. "Your mother knew it might come to this. You need to lock me in."

They stood in silence for a moment while Jade contemplated what her father asked. This prison was designed for him; to keep him locked away for the safety of the universe. She knew it was necessary, but she'd lost one parent today and didn't want to lose another.

"Father, please."
Her father turned to her, the black eyes fading a little to show some of the man beneath. "Jade, you have to do this. You have to lock me in there."

"Then what?" she enquired painfully. "Go back to Xenfar? Go back to school?"

His face took on a grave concern. "No, Jade. Never go back there. The people who want me will come for you, and they'll start there."

"But grandfather—"

"No one can stop them, Jade. You need to run and hide. Find a backwater world and lay low, blend in."

The suppressed heat from the sun around them was still scorching. It baked Jade's face like an intense sauna as she stared at her father. "I can't do this alone. Please, come with me. We can find a way to help you," she pleaded, knowing the answer already.

He fixed Jade with a serious stare. "I can't, Jade; I could hurt people. I could hurt you. I couldn't forgive myself."

Without another word, he hugged her, gripping her tightly before releasing Jade and walking away. Opening the chamber, he entered slowly, turning to look at Jade before closing it. "Lock this door and take the key with you, Jade. Keep it safe for me."

She nodded as she watched her father close himself in. A childish urge to run to him, to stop him, almost got the best of her as she forced herself to step forward to lock the door. The key was a slim silver thing, subtly made. Its home was set into the door at the height of her head, lined with graphic motifs.

With a heavy heart, Jade pushed the key into the slot and turned. The graphic images immediately lit up with a blue glow as various mechanical sounds could be heard from behind the stone and metal. Her job completed, she withdrew the key, placing it around her neck on its silver chain. Then, right there, in the middle of this arcane temple her mother had built, she let herself break down. Falling to the floor, she curled into a ball and cried.

She was alone in the universe…and hunted.

WHAT IF?
MOLLIE ANNE GATES

It started with a tiny crack only as wide as a little finger.
That's all it was. At first.

HISSSSSSS!

Gas from deep inside the star seeped out.
The oldest star in the universe was doomed.
"No!" it shouted, struggling to hold itself together.
But it couldn't.

BANG! BANG! BANG!

The star died.
Extreme heat and blinding light poured out into the universe.
Bits of the shattered star were flung into the deep darkness of space.
The jagged pieces smashed into one another.
Only dust remained from what had once been
the oldest star in the universe.

Over years, too many to count, the dust drifted until it lost interest in
space travel.
It had witnessed new planets born in blazes of light.
It had lost its way in a darkness no light could enter.
What had once seemed new and surprising felt like every day events.

The stardust wondered: "What if there is more to life than this?"

It asked comets zooming by. And tumbling asteroids.
Falling stars were difficult to keep up with,
so the dust asked as quickly as possible.
None had an answer.

None had thought of such a question before.

After all, the comets were hard at work,
streaking through the universe.
Asteroids were busy tumbling.
Being a falling star was dizzying.
Comets and asteroids and falling stars had no free time
in which to ask questions or ponder esoteric ideas.

Unlike the stardust.

Unable to find an answer to its question, the stardust contemplated
giving up.
Talking with comets and asteroids was boring.
They had nothing new to say. The dust rushed to get out of the way of
falling stars.
They only wanted to talk about speed.

What if there were no answer to the stardust's question?
Or what if floating was all there was to life?

No longer caring where it was or where it was going,
the stardust drifted, not bothering to talk with comets or asteroids,
much less falling stars.
Until the wind, gusting and howling, blew by.

"You look sad," the wind said. "And you're drifting."
"You're right. I am sad," the stardust said.
"Is there anything I can do to help?" the wind asked,
slowing to a gentle breeze.

The stardust said, "Everywhere I look, I see what I've already seen
before."
"I see," the wind said, moaning and sighing.
More than anything, he wanted to find an answer for his new friend.

The wind grew very powerful when it was thinking.
The stardust said, "That's all right. I've given up finding an answer."
It feared it would be scattered across the universe
if the wind didn't calm down.

Calm down is exactly what the wind did next. It'd found an answer!

Barely rippling, the wind exclaimed, "Look below you!"
"It's a bright blue-and-green planet," the stardust said.
"Yes. But it's also shiny because it's the answer to your question."
"What?"
The stardust was more confused than ever.

"I blew by it before gusting up here," the wind said.
"That planet is looking for its first child. It could be you!"
"What is a child? How could I become one?" the stardust asked.
"Let's find out," the wind answered.
"What's the planet's name?"
"Earth," the wind said.

What if the stardust did become a child?
A child who grew into an astronaut and traveled far out into space.
What if the astronaut grew old and, one night, fell into a deep sleep?
In that slumber, she dreamt of seeing the universe's oldest star
shattered into dust.

Stardust.

In her dream, the bang was so loud her eardrums popped.
Her teeth rattled until her head felt like it were rolling off her shoulders.
The dream was as clear and sharp as if the astronaut had been there.

What if?

INFINITY HOTEL
DOROTHY TINKER

"Can you imagine? Bathtubs the size of pools! Infinite room service! Every entertainment channel you can imagine!" The man in the seat beside me pauses to gasp in air and breathes, "And the price!"

I only nod and glance down at the brochure in my hand. *The Infinity Hotel*, it proclaims. *Infinite Dimensions catering to the needs of every soul.*

I tap the glossy paper idly with one finger and let my eyes drift to the porthole beside me. A bright darkness meets my gaze, and strange stars appear to dance just on the other side.

My contemplation of the unfamiliar starscape is interrupted by a heavy grip on my shoulder. "Oy! Aren't you excited?" demands the man beside me.

I roll my eyes at the dancing stars, which appear to twinkle in amusement, before turning my head to meet the man's stare.

"Not particularly," I answer. "It's just another resort."

"Just another resort?" he snaps in disbelief. He raises his fist, his copy of the brochure rolled up within it. "How can you say that? It's the most high-tech hotel in the *galaxy!*"

I tap the brochure against my thigh this time and shake my head. "I'm an entertainment reviewer. I've seen every kind of resort and hotel you can think of, from the run-down Motel Ones on Sol 2 to the opulent Crystal Rivers of the Orion Belt. I've even taken a time leap to the End of Time Resort. I doubt this 'Infinity' Hotel can do better than anything else I've seen."

The man stares at me for a long moment before shaking his head back and forth. "But none of those could possibly be as cheap as a single credit per room."

I refrain from rolling my eyes again and offer him a wry smile. "Cheap is exactly what I'm afraid of."

"Why?"

Glancing up, my smile becomes truer as I spy a pair of wide eyes peering between the headrests of the seats in front of me.

"Why what?" I ask the young girl.

"Why would you be afraid of—?"

"Oh, don't pester the man, Nellie," a harried voice speaks up from beside the girl, and Nellie pulls her face back from the space between the seats.

"But, Mammy…"

"I don't mind," I speak up before the elderly woman—surely the girl's grandmother—can chastise her again. "I just wanted to clarify what she was asking."

"Oh, well…"

"You said you were afraid of cheap," the girl continues as her grandmother falls silent. "Mammy says that we're only able to afford to go to the Infinity Hotel because it's so cheap, so why would you go there if you were afraid of cheap?"

I chuckle gently. "I meant cheap in quality, not necessarily cost. I know the brochures claim this Infinity Hotel is high-tech, but I don't see how that can be possible when they are charging their guests so little."

The man beside me begins to splutter, but a woman speaks up from the row behind us.

"If the Infinity Hotel were really so low in quality, would they have invited an entertainment reviewer with your experience to come stay with them?"

Glancing back, I raise my eyebrows in surprise. The woman now leaning against the back of my seat shows no signs of the technology I'm accustomed to seeing around most people every day. She wears her dark hair in a simple braid. Her ears and face are both unadorned, marred only by a couple of scars that most women I know would have already had removed with surgery. Even her clothes appear to be hand-stitched rather than laser-made.

"Are you Cylian?" I ask.

She nods and offers me a small smile. "I am. I'm—"

"What's Cylian?" the young girl in front of me asks.

"Nellie!" her grandmother hisses. "That's rude!"

"But, Mammy…" the girl whines.

As the grandmother continues to chastise the girl, I shake my head and turn my full attention to the Cylian woman behind me.

"What's a Cylian doing on a trip to the galaxy's 'most high-tech' hotel resort? I thought the Cylians avoided excess technology as much as possible."

She nods, but a frown tugs at her lips. "We do. I'm not quite sure why I'm here, except that I know this is where I should be."

"What—?" I begin to ask, but another voice, gentle and feminine, sounds through the speaker system.

"Good evening, honored guests. The transport will be docking at the Infinity Hotel within moments. When you arrive, the hotel's guardians will begin the registration process. Once each of you is registered, you will be directed to your initial room. On behalf of the Infinite Dimensions, we hope you enjoy your stay with us."

As the voice falls silent, a soft *click* echoes through the cabin, quickly followed by a soft *hiss* as the entire right wall slides open. The man beside me quickly tumbles out, his head already snapping from side to side. In the seat behind him, a gray-haired man sighs wearily, smoothing his hands down the front of his immaculate suit before following.

Nellie's grandmother ushers the girl out next, muttering worriedly. As she bustles Nellie after the two men, a single woman steps from the front seat, her gaze distant as she scans the rest of the transport and the dock. I don't know what she is looking for, but she gives a small sniff before striding after the others.

"I wonder why they only bring seven people at a time?" the Cylian woman murmurs.

"What do you mean?" I ask as I stand up and stretch. It's more out of habit than necessity; my legs don't feel sore like they usually do after an extended trip.

"Well, there was no lack of people waiting to visit the Infinity Hotel, and the brochures claim the hotel has an infinite number of rooms, yet there is only one transport with seven seats to bring visitors into the dimension. Don't you find that strange?"

I pause with one foot on the floor of the dock and turn to frown at the Cylian. "Waiting? I don't remember standing in line."

She shrugs. "We may not have, but I saw plenty of people hoping to make the next transport."

I shake my head. "Maybe they were waiting for a different destination." I don't wait to hear her response.

Instead, I stride out onto the dock, hoping to catch up with the others as quickly as possible. I'm so focused that I don't realize until I'm nearly halfway down the hallway that the walls around me shimmer. Glancing to the right, I pause mid-stride and stare.

What I originally thought to be the reflection of light off metal (steel, gold, or otherwise) turns out to be the flutter of wings and the glow of a sunset. Stepping closer, I watch, amazed, as a large, fiery bird stretches its wings and then launches itself toward the scarlet horizon.

"Splendid Phoenicia, keeper of the star cycles and protector of souls."

I turn, startled. The Cylian watches the image of the sunset with a small smile.

"'Protector of souls'?" I ask, doubtful. "It looks like the firebirds of the Ankaa system."

The Cylian turns her smile to me. "Have you never heard the old Sol legends?"

I shake my head. "I'm an entertainment reviewer, not a historian."

She nods, her smile never changing. "The phoenix was said to be long-lived, and even when it died, the fires of its death would rebirth it. Its flames are said to be born of the stars themselves, reflecting their cycles. Its never-ending life protects the souls of all living things."

I shake my head. "That sounds like religion to me. I try to stay away from such things."

The Cylian tilts her head and meets my gaze with a curious quirk of her lips. "Very well," she murmurs after a long moment. "Then perhaps we should continue on."

I nod and stride down the hallway. I glance at the walls as I go, but while I see other beautiful landscapes, nothing catches my attention like the firebird did.

We are just entering the hotel lobby when a loud cry drives me to speed up my steps. "I don't want to go by myself!" I hear Nellie scream.

"Please!" her grandmother begs. "We're poor. Surely you can give us a single room to share."

"My apologies, madam," answers a gentle voice that sounds very similar to the one we heard on the transport. "Our rules are simple: one guest per room, one credit per room. You may not share."

"Mammy!" Nellie screams, and I wince at the pitch of the girl's voice. "Don't let them!"

Nellie's grandmother glances around uncertainly, but she and her granddaughter stand alone with a man I assume is one of the hotel's guardians. Her eyes light up when she spots me, but I shake my head, knowing already that I won't be able to influence the situation. If the rules are as strict as the guardian insists…

"Can you explain why two people cannot share a room, guardian?" the Cylian woman asks.

The guardian—a young-looking man with warm brown skin, pale hair that appears to glow in the lobby's lighting, and dressed in a white uniform—nods serenely.

"Each room is calibrated to measure the needs of its occupant so that we can provide appropriate upgrades when necessary. If we allowed two people to share a room, then the needs of one guest would interfere with the needs of the other and any upgrades would fit neither guest."

"Upgrades?" I ask, curious despite my earlier disinterest.

"Oh yes," the guardian affirms. "There are seven initial rooms, one for each new arrival. These evaluate each guest's needs between registration and the next wave of arrivals. The guests are then moved to rooms that are more appropriate to their needs. Every time the needs of a guest change, he or she is upgraded to a more appropriate room."

"Oh, dear," Nellie's grandmother mutters, wringing her hands. "A credit per room. Are we charged for each move?"

The guardian offers her a gentle smile. "Yes, madam, but you needn't worry. Number of credits is part of the needs that are considered during the evaluation process. A guest is never upgraded more often than they can afford."

The guardian's words don't appear to soothe Nellie's grandmother, and she glances at Nellie, who stares at the guardian in fascination, all signs of her earlier tears erased. "If Nellie isn't with me," the grandmother asks, "then how will she be able to pay for any upgrades?"

"There is no need to worry about that, madam," the guardian answers. "Even children have enough credits to afford several upgrades."

As though to prove his point, he brushes his fingertips against Nellie's forehead, which gently glows a deep indigo for a moment before a small, golden number appears in the same spot.

"How...?"

I'm not sure who whispers the question (it might have been me, for all my surprise), but the number disappears quickly, and the guardian turns patient eyes on the grandmother.

"Do you have any more questions, madam?"

She shakes her head wordlessly, and Nellie gives a squeal and reaches for the guardian's hand. Taking her hand, he brushes a single finger against her forehead and then leads her to one of the hallways that leads off the lobby. Glancing around, I realize that it is one of seven hallways, not counting the one we just walked in from.

"One hallway for each new arrival," the Cylian woman murmurs. "Each one must contain the initial room the guardian mentioned."

I nod and watch as the guardian opens a door just inside the hallway he's chosen. Nellie soon gives another squeal and disappears inside, leaving the guardian to softly close the door behind her.

With the little girl secured in her room, the grandmother goes to her own quietly, though she continues to wring her hands even as she steps through the door that the guardian holds open for her. As the door slides shut behind her, the guardian turns back to me and the Cylian woman and offers a smooth bow.

"If you would join me, honored guests, I will show you to the remaining initial rooms."

We meet him at the mouth of the next hallway. When he glances between us, I step back and wave a hand toward the Cylian woman, who gives me a small smile and bows her head toward the guardian. He brushes one finger against her forehead, and from this distance, I can see the small burst of indigo that accompanies the gesture.

Before I can consider asking about it, the guardian turns to the nearby door and slips it open. As the Cylian woman murmurs her thanks and steps inside, I peek around her, once again more curious than I had been throughout the journey here. Through the doorway, I spy the foot of a large bed overflowing with blankets and pillows and a wall that appears to be dominated by the latest in personal entertainment technology. I briefly wonder how comfortable the Cylian woman will be surrounded by such excess before the door slides shut and the guardian turns to me.

Now that I'm familiar with the process, I don't wait for the guardian to direct me. Instead, I turn to the next hallway, the last one before the door-less hallway through which we'd entered the lobby. When I stop by the first door and turn back to the guardian, I find him watching me with a small quirk of his lips.

"Eager to explore, sir?" he asks, even as he lifts his hand and brushes his finger against my forehead (oddly, I don't see the indigo light this time).

"Just curious," I answer before stepping through the now-open doorway.

I hardly notice the guardian closing the door as I take in the room. To my left is a wall dominated by vivid, three-dimensional holographic images that somehow manage to appear unobtrusive for all that they fill most of the wall. A quick glance is enough for me to ascertain the presence of holograms associated with video systems, game systems, music systems, and even an interactive system for live events.

To my right is a bed nearly twice as large as I had imagined from the glimpse I got of the Cylian's room. Stepping up to it, I run a hand over the tumble of blankets and pillows and close my eyes in pleasure. The sheets are of the lightest silks from the Comae system, the blankets of the softest wools from the Hamal system, and while I can't see the feathers that stuff the pillows, I would hazard that they come from the finest birds of the Apodis system.

Forcing myself away from the bed after one final squeeze of the closest pillow (sleeping will certainly not be a burden), I step farther into the room. On the other side of the bed, a double-sided bookshelf juts out from the wall, its shelves filled with tomes ranging in age from the classics of the old Sol system to the more modern Thousand-Dimension Explorations series that has been the entertainment business's obsession for the past few years. I spend a moment noting several titles I wish to enjoy later before I step past.

Here is a dining table that can produce any dish one might ask for. There is the bathroom my aisle-mate gushed over during the transport journey, with its oversized tub, multitude of bathing soaps, bubbles, and accessories, and a shower that cleans with actual water (versus the sonic and pressure showers that have become more prevalent within the last few centuries).

Staring around the bathroom, I shake my head slowly. Despite the apparent opulence of the room, I feel…heavy. It's almost an ache in my chest, and I realize, as I turn back to the rest of the room, that something's missing. I'm not sure what that something might be, but it's not there and I find myself filled with a deepening disappointment.

After that, I simply wander the room. I don't touch the entertainment systems—I've spent too long reviewing these for them to hold any interest for me. I pick up the books that sound interesting, only to once again put them aside. I order a simple meal of Siribeast and Spican plains vegetables from the dining table but am too restless to eat more than half. The same is true for the bed as I spend perhaps five or fifteen minutes among its grasping mounds before I find myself prowling the room once more.

I don't know how long this lasts (at some point, I discover that there are no time-keeping devices of any kind within the room). It is only the sound of a gentle knock that breaks me from my unsettled wandering. A sudden determination, equal in strength to the restlessness I've been feeling, springs up within me, and I stride eagerly for the door.

The guardian who greets me is not the one who showed me to my room earlier. This one appears older, and he doesn't smile, though his expression is still gentle. He directs my gaze farther down the hallway with a sweep of one hand and a murmured "Your upgrades are ready."

I bite the inside of my cheek to prevent the snapping response that wants to break free and step into the hallway. Before I can take more than a couple of steps though, a familiar voice breaks through my restless haze.

"What do you mean I have to upgrade? This was only supposed to cost a single credit!"

Frowning, I step back toward the lobby, ignoring my guardian's murmured protest. Leaning around the corner—I feel oddly averse to actually stepping *into* the lobby—I spy my former aisle-mate arguing with his guardian just inside one of the other hallways.

"I am sorry, sir," his guardian answers, sounding very much like the guardian who originally showed us to our rooms. "The rules of the Infinity Hotel dictate at least one upgrade. This initial room was only to measure your needs that we might form your next room to best fulfill them."

My former aisle-mate scowls. "This room fits me well enough! I don't see why I should move, especially when I don't want to spend the extra credit. The brochure advertised this place as a credit per room. I expect to pay no more than that!"

His guardian bows his head. "I understand, sir. If you wish to pay no more than a single credit during this stay, then you can always move on from the Infinite Dimensions. Your stay here is not required."

The man grimaces and glances farther down his hallway. His hands alternate between clenching into fists and relaxing, and his jaw works back and forth. After a moment of watching him, I pull my head back and turn to my guardian.

"Would I be able to pay for that man's first upgrade?"

My guardian blinks. "You would wish to?"

I shrug. "It's only a credit, and he was so excited about coming here, much more than I was. I would hate to see him give up on it just because he had to upgrade when he didn't want to."

My guardian hums softly as his eyes drop to one side. "Such charity…" he murmurs. After a moment, he nods and meets my gaze. "It is possible for you to make such an offer to him. Personally, I would not recommend to him that he take it, but no matter his response, the offer will…affect your own upgrades."

I frown. "How so?"

My guardian opens his mouth and then hesitates, his head turning toward the lobby. Almost immediately, he steps out of my hallway, and I lean back around the corner to watch him stride toward my former aisle-mate, catching the man's shoulder just as he's about to step into the lobby.

"Do not be so hasty in your decision, sir," my guardian says when the other man glares at him. "One of our other guests has offered to pay the necessary credit for your first upgrade."

The other guardian stiffens and glances at mine, wide-eyed. Before he can speak whatever protests he holds, his charge grins and exclaims, "I'll take it then!"

I roll my eyes and turn around to lean back against the wall. The restlessness from before has returned, and I clench and unclench my fists in hopes of relieving it. Unfortunately, such a gesture is as useless as wandering my previous room was.

"Come."

I start and open my eyes. My guardian is standing in front of me, one hand resting gently on my shoulder. When I meet his eyes, he nods farther down my hallway and murmurs, "Your upgrade will help calm you."

I frown, wondering how he knows what I'm feeling, but I don't resist as he shepherds me down the corridor. We soon come to an intersection with another hallway, and he pauses. After what feels like a minute of stillness, I glance at him and realize that he is watching me with patient eyes.

"What?"

"I am afraid some decision is required on your part."

I glance at the intersection, but none of the three directions appears to be unique. Turning back to him, I mutter, "What kind of decision?"

"Which feels more appropriate?"

I frown. "Which feels more appropriate? What kind of question is that?"

The guardian tilts his chin down. "I did say that your charity would affect your upgrades. This is part of that."

I don't understand what he means, but I glance in each direction again. Once more there is no visual difference, so I close my eyes and step into the intersection. Taking a deep breath, I focus on how I feel.

The heaviness in my chest is strong, but as I think about it in relation to the hallways, I find myself leaning toward the right.

Literally.

Opening my eyes, I stumble to the right, only the guardian's sudden grip on my shoulders preventing me from tumbling to the ground.

"What the…?"

"You made your decision," is all my guardian says, and he leads the way.

There are no more words between us as he guides me to a door, brushes his fingers against my forehead, and helps me inside. It isn't until the door slides shut behind me that I realize he is no longer with me.

Shaking my head to rid myself of my confused haze, I glance around the new room. Almost immediately, I release a heavy breath and simply stare.

The room holds a bed with the finest of materials and a food-producing dining table, but the similarities to my original room seem to end there. The bed is much smaller, just large enough for me to sprawl across comfortably, and the blankets and pillows accompanying it are much more modest in number and size. The wall of entertainment systems is gone, replaced by walls of bookshelves and still lifes and landscapes. The bathroom is also more modest in size and appliances. The tub is more reasonable for a single person, and the small number of soaps that line its edge are of scents that I favor.

The most striking difference, however, is the glass door that lets out into what appears to be an open-air garden.

Stepping through, I stare at the riot of colors that surround me. Greens, reds, purples, blues, pinks, and more colors that I can only compare to stars and sunsets and exotic creatures that I've only ever seen in photographs.

"How?" I breathe. The garden is small, barely three full steps across and perhaps seven deep, but it appears to rival the Crystal Rivers of the Orion Belt in its beauty.

I don't know how long I stand there, staring at the flowers and enjoying the signs of life that fill such a cramped space. I feel no hunger as I watch them, and no desire to sleep. I only feel a lightness within my chest.

I'm just beginning to stir and wonder what else there might be when a soft knock reaches my ears. Blinking, I turn from the plants and stumble back into the room, grimacing as I'm met with colors so dull the items they belong to are hard to discern.

Once the door to the hallway is open, I simply stand there, blinking up at the guardian who awaits me. This one appears to be a young woman, and I wonder briefly why my last guardian didn't return.

"If you'll come with me, sir," she murmurs, "your next upgrades are ready."

I wonder for a moment about the parts of my current room that I didn't explore, but one glance over my shoulder cures me of such thoughts. It's too dull for me to consider returning to anything but the garden.

When this guardian leads me to an intersection as well, I frown at her. "I thought the rooms were specifically calibrated to figure out the needs of the guests."

"They are."

I raise one eyebrow. "Then this is...?"

She has the decency to blush. "I'm afraid you added this element when you offered to pay for another guest's upgrades. Charity is...costly...you could say."

I cross my arms. "How is charity costly?"

She bites her lip and glances away from me, and I'm struck by the fact that she seems to be younger than any of the other guardians I've met so far.

"Well," she whispers, "if you think of credits as currency, then...charity is quite costly to the giver."

I blink. I consider mentioning that I only gave away one credit to pay for the other man's first upgrade, but something about her words seems more important.

"Credits are the accepted form of payment throughout the galaxy. What would they be if not a form of currency?"

She tilts her head and meets my gaze so steadily and directly that I suddenly wonder why I thought she seemed young only moments ago. Now, I see only confidence and knowledge in her eyes.

"You ask the right questions, don't you?" I blink, confused, but she continues before I can ask what she means. "You must remember that we are in the Infinite Dimensions, not the galaxy you know."

"Yes, it's a separate dimension. I thought that was why you were able to have an 'Infinity' Hotel in the first place."

She shakes her head. "You misunderstand me. The Infinite Dimensions are not just a separate dimension from the galaxy you know. They are *beyond* the galaxy you know."

Beyond…

My throat tightens. I raise a hand to touch my throat, but I know it'll do no good. "Beyond…how?" I manage to choke out.

The guardian doesn't smile, but like the others, her expression is oh, so gentle.

"Beyond the life you've known. Beyond the life any of you have known."

I grunt, and distantly, I'm aware that I have fallen back against a wall. It's hardly important against the guardian's words and the fact that I've just learned…

I shake my head. "I…don't…remember…"

"And you won't," she answers. Her voice is deeper than before, and I lift my gaze to find her staring at me with eyes that look much wiser and older than I had originally seen. "The end is not what is important in the life you knew. The journey and the experiences that made it up are most important."

"The experiences," I whisper. "Like the rooms?"

She nods. "The upgrades are continuations of the experiences of the life you knew. In that life, you collected and shed burdens on your soul. When you come beyond that life, you bear those burdens with you. We here in the Infinite Dimensions have found it easier to refer to these burdens as currency in order to ease the transition from that life into this one."

She tilts her head again and watches me with those deepening eyes. "Most souls never realize what the Infinite Dimensions are. Some remain and find their way to clearing the burdens from their souls. Those that do are allowed to move beyond and make their place among the community of unburdened souls.

"Many others, however, move on from the Infinite Dimensions altogether and back into the galaxy that you knew."

My earlier aversion to return to the lobby suddenly comes to mind. "That's why my earlier guardian stopped the other man from stepping into the lobby, isn't it? If he had returned to the lobby, he would have...what? Been reincarnated?"

She tilts her head slightly. "That is the word that many use for the renewal of the soul in the galaxy you know. It is more of a rebirth than a reincarnation, though. The soul is burned and purged of burdens and many other things that make it who it arrived here as previously."

I shiver. "I'm not much for religions, but that sounds more like passing through a form of Hell to return to the living."

The guardian offers me a wry smile. "Not all religions made up their beliefs."

I shake my head and turn back to the intersection, suddenly determined not to give up on the Infinity Hotel. "You said earlier that charity is costly. Does that mean that these intersections increase the number of burdens I clear from my soul?"

"They can. Or they can simply determine which burdens you clear. Charity on your part adds...unpredictability to the Infinite Dimensions."

I laugh. It's so sudden that I pause, but the guardian is already nodding.

"Unpredictability is what you need, I believe." Waving toward the intersection, she adds, "Now choose."

And I do.

THE ANGEL OF MONDAYS
D. MARIE PROKOP

A tomcat named Whiskers prowled the suburban landscape. Suddenly, the sleek, black feline stopped in its tracks, lowered itself back on its haunches, and stared into space. Only, it wasn't just space. The joggers, kids on bikes, and shirtless men mowing their lawns did not see anything out of the ordinary, but animal senses being superior in this regard, the observant cat saw an astounding sight.

Whiskers's green eyes narrowed as he witnessed the arrival of two enormous celestial beings, their luminescence far beyond the spectrum of human vision. The cat's eyes reflected the opalescent shine of two magnificent angels landing in the cul-de-sac.

The heavenly warriors each folded one set of white wings flat against their muscular backs. A second set of wings fluttered to rest over their feet. One of the warriors winked at Whiskers.

"You have a new assignment," the darker-skinned one said, conversing telepathically.

The second being, light-skinned and golden-haired, replied without moving his lips. "Which is?"

"You will be notified step-by-step. Prepare yourself thus."

Whiskers could sense the mood of the strange visitors' conversation, but without audio, the cat resigned itself to merely observing. A young boy on a neon orange bicycle flew past, causing the fur on Whiskers's back to ripple. A lawnmower was exchanged for a leaf blower in the yard up front as the two angelic beings continued their silent discourse under Whiskers's watchful eye.

"Why me?"

"The defining event takes place on a Monday. You are Zaniel, angel of Mondays, correct?"

"Yes, Michael, I am. I suppose Mondays *are* my thing. But if you think about it, my name means nothing, you know, compared to the Name above all names. To be honest, I often wonder about Tuesdays."

The darker heavenly being responded with a facial expression best described as *stoic*. Indeed, the archangel Michael's tawny features, rugged jaw, and rippling muscles all contributed to the fear he struck in his demonic opponents.

Zaniel inhaled and became respectfully demure. He lowered his blue eyes. A slight twinkle hid behind a veil of thick lashes.

"I will be prepared, Michael. You may notify Him thus."

"Zaniel, this assignment can only be accomplished through you."

"You've forgotten something," Zaniel replied, his eyes looking away from Michael and landing upon Whiskers.

"We cannot *forget* things," Michael corrected.

"Yes, sir, bad choice of words. English is a complicated language…I only meant to point out that we have no power over one thing—the one thing I have never understood."

Michael glowered at Zaniel, his coal black eyes turning as dark as a night devoid of stars.

"We know much and have glorious power. Of what 'thing' do you speak?"

Zaniel replied, "The human will."

Michael stooped down and examined a wildflower growing in the shade. He looked up at Zaniel.

"What did Adam name this?"

It was framed like a test question. Whiskers, noticing the pause in the conversation, perked up. After a pregnant pause, Zaniel answered his commander.

"Ah. I have studied man since his beginning. Adam was asked to name the animals, not the plants, so it is not surprising that he nicknamed this flower *Eagle's Claw*. But the descendants of Adam have given it the scientific name *Aquilegia vulgaris*."

His commander, the archangel, did not appear either impressed or unimpressed. Michael's expression never wavered as he asked his next question.

"And does it have a common name, another one derived from the Latin perhaps?"

Zaniel smiled. His liquid blue eyes sparkled. *Ah, Latin, a truly beautiful, succinct language.*

"*Columbine*," Zaniel replied, the melodic word flowing from his mind.

"*Aquilegia*—resembling an eagle's claw, as Adam saw it. Or *Columbine*— meaning 'dove.' Well, Zaniel, is this flower like an eagle's claw or a cluster of doves?"

"What do *you* see?" Zaniel dared to ask.

"Hmmm…you answer like the Son, with a question. It is both." Michael paused, admiring the purple and pink petals of the earthly plant at his feet. A look of compassion crossed Michael's face when he continued. "Zaniel, humans are incomprehensible. There are magnificent forces around them, and yet they seem unaware of His glory. Here it is, proclaimed by this complex flower, and they confess their ignorance by naming it with dichotomous terms. This flower is actually toxic. Like humans after the Fall, it has a dual nature. But see how it hangs its head? It bows humbly before its Creator."

"It looks sad," Zaniel observed.

His commander's eyes blazed with fire. Michael turned his gaze toward the plant. It shriveled, reduced to gray ash. Whiskers sneezed.

"Dust to dust. Remember that, Zaniel. This world is temporary. It will perish in fire and flame. It is the things that do not perish—love, hope, and peace—that are everlasting. These are the things we are sent to fight for."

"Am I to smite humans?" Zaniel asked. He had been wanting to do that for centuries.

"No. The war continues on. We follow our orders and never question the Authority under which they are given. We are not human."

Zaniel nodded, acknowledging his status as a mere foot soldier in the war.

Michael continued. "In contrast to the human will, angels have a singular nature. We obey. The love of God compels us without interference or distractions. Humans must choose to obey. Over and over and over."

Whiskers blinked. The bright orange bike sped by again, its rider's face filled with childish glee. Michael's stern face softened and then rallied. With effervescent pride, he finished his speech.

"Yahweh's love is strong. Though incomprehensible to us, the human's ability to choose, though it makes failure a possibility, was part of Yahweh's design. It is also what makes love, hope, and peace possible for the sons of Adam."

"I am at Yahweh's command. Praise His Holy Name!"

"Praise the Holy One! Zaniel, I must depart from you now. There is a battle I must wage."

Zaniel's playful eyes danced as he broke away from the messy language they had conversed in up until now and offered his farewell.

"*¡Adiós!*"

Being closer to Latin's simplicity, Zaniel felt more comfortable conversing in español, even telepathically. But the gravelly voice of his superior did not return a poetic word of farewell, in any language.

Instead, the fierce angelic warrior replied, "We will continue this conversation after I crush certain demon heads into sulfuric pulp."

"*¡Vaya con Dios!*"

Michael acknowledged Zaniel's benediction with a sturdy nod and unfurled both sets of wings.

After the archangel soared up into the infinite blue sky, Whiskers approached Zaniel, not intimidated in the least by the effervescent glory surrounding the awesome being. Zaniel stroked the fluffy, ebony fur on Whiskers's back. Being touched by the gentle heavenly force caused Whiskers to purr uncontrollably loud.

Despite the cat's pleasant companionship, the cacophony of noises in the broken world surrounding him rattled the lone angel. There were some ruinous places on the earth, terrible places, places in which Zaniel feared to tread.

Zaniel, a faithful soldier of God, spent all his Mondays away from home. He reminisced about his days in heaven, when morning and night he would worship the Almighty with joy and awe, in respite from the war.

He yearned for the day this undisclosed assignment would end. Zaniel, angel of Mondays, longed…for Tuesday.

TESTIMONY
PETER VENABLE

A tectonic shift severs a mountain face from a Canary Island volcano;
the colossal landslide propels fifty-foot Leviathan jaws toward coasts…

magma under the Yellowstone Caldera explodes;
an ash plume lathers the earth and jells in lung cavities…

a three-mile, tumbling asteroid collides with Antarctica,
blows ice flakes and penguin atoms up thirty miles…

axis and allied men launch their nuclear missiles,
pulverizing matter into mushroom clouds spilling radioactive rain…

prayers evaporate like rivers and lakes into bloodshot smoke
as monoliths collapse into rubble and ruin…

a rider Faithful and True, eyes flaming like fire,
pilots a celestial horse with armies following:

"Yes, I am coming, soon!" (Rev. 22:20)

ASTRAL BODY
CHANTELL RENEE

"The man from Mars is through with cars..." Beth sang along with the music in her earpiece. None of her devices indicated any new buried treasures in the desolate land she'd decided to pick over today. "He's gonna eat 'em all, hmm hmm..." She didn't know all the words, so she hummed along. "I think this place used to be Texas! Miles of flat open space and tumbleweeds. I swear, I see an actual cactus around the edge of that mountain."

Looking up, she saw a pale blue sky with thin, white clouds smeared here and there. She'd never seen such a thing. Beth stood still and took a moment to commit it to memory. The light from the rising sun started to warm the skin of her face. She knew she couldn't stay too much longer now.

"Beth, your readings are showing radiation contamination will hit critical levels in three minutes." The artificial voice of her ship's computer system interrupted the music in her earpiece.

Ugh! "Okay, Sissy!" One last eye-full. *This had to have been Texas.* She reached down and snatched up a rock to take with her.

The force field that hugged her skin kept the radiated stone from harming her. Beth had at least 0.5 Kilograms of Earth rocks already. *What damage could one more do?* She laughed to herself.

"Sissy, let's head to the lunar rock on our way out," Beth said as she climbed the ramp to her ship, tossing the rock into the "scavenged" bin that held a few hunks of metal and wire. The tiny worker bots would lift that all on board, and then they could leave. Once she reached the top, she passed through the ship's protective field and was able to deactivate her personal fields.

"Beth, it is not allowable by the Federal Star Regent to land on a disintegrating astral body."

"Who said anything about landing? Sissy, just bypass that dumb regulation, and clear all system logs of my activity since we entered this solar system."

"Yes, Beth."

Darn, she didn't even put up a fight. Beth would update the latest regulations when she got back, which would give her a few months of challenging banter. *It's fun to have someone to bicker with.*

She used to be able to do this with her family, but now they simply ignored Beth. She'd left well enough alone with them. It was one thing to break away from the norm, another to become a nuisance and be seen as a threat.

As soon as she got back on the main deck, she switched off autopilot. It was best to manually fly through the debris in this part of space. Once the ship was off the blue planet, the next destination came quickly.

Much of one side of the moon had been destroyed by the bombs. All the shattered pieces had finally made a real ring around Earth, but a decent chunk of the white lunar surface remained. The scan of it showed nothing new. The radiation readings were still high even though it had been close to eight-hundred years since the nuclear explosions. Beth maneuvered the ship to go, but something shiny caught her eye.

"Sissy, analyze the reflective surface I'm seeing."

"Okay, Beth. It is a metal object. It could be a pole, a piece of a craft, or a case containing something. It has volume, and appears to be 180 centimeters in length and two square meters in area."

"Hmmm, let's get a little closer."

The inside of the moon was as white as its surface. The object was lodged in the center of a great hole in the middle of the astral body.

"Sissy, deploy the bots and program them to bring all parts of the object to decontamination for inspection. And make sure you fine tune their settings; I don't want them cutting up the object, just the rock it's lodged in."

"This area is a highly flammable. The Federal Star Regent…"

"Got it, Sissy! My father can shove it! Deactivate their beams if you're so worried."

Beth twisted around in her chair to watch as a dozen or more of the small round metal robots made their way to the object. They worked in small groups, tapping out the rock and loosening the shiny cylinder. Once free, the long silver pod-shaped thing floated freely in space. Something about the pod tickled at Beth's memory. The bots gently guided the object towards the ship.

"Easy as pie!" Beth smiled.

"Decontamination complete. Will you be inspecting it now?"

"No, let's get on home first. Sissy, you drive."

Beth hit a button that activated the music she'd compiled for flying. The sound of instruments filled the cabin; classical music it was called. Beth leaned back and let her mind drift.

Seventy-six hours later, the ship docked at a space station, another relic Beth had recovered. It'd been floating in the Milky Way, lost and in need of repair. She had gutted it of all inferior technology and replaced it with the fusion of technology her family had discovered as they grew and spread from solar system to solar system.

"Rocket man…" Beth sang as she moved through to her living area aboard the refurbished station. She'd made the walls blue like Earth's sky and the floors brown like the ground. Sissy gave the tiny robots orders as Beth kicked off her dusty boots and let down the thick coils of hair she'd let grow.

Her family would think she was crazy for having the hair at all. But she enjoyed how it felt and looked. As she relaxed, her body morphed into her natural form. A new guitar riff filled the room from an actual stereo speaker she'd found on one of her scavenging adventures.

"Hmm hmmm, New Orleans…brown sugar…" she sang along. The data storages she found had various songs and had become one of her favorite finds.

"All items have been brought inside." Sissy's voice announced.

"Well then, let's see what we've found."

The bots placed the silver cylinder in the medical bay. Beth stepped into the small, clean space. All of the walls and floor were medical-grade porcelain, but its impressive gleam paled to that of the silver of what she could clearly see was a pod. On its surface was a hand depression.

"Five fingers, silver escape pod, could this be…" She let her limb re-adjust for the device and pressed her hand onto the scanner.

This had to be one of *the* silver pods. *What luck!* She could scarcely contain her excitement. The hand-shaped plate glowed green. The color spread across the upper part of the cylinder. It split in two, down the center, and opened. Just as she was about to get a look, the little bots came out of the walls and turned red.

"Organic matter detected. Radiation contamination may occur." Sissy's mechanical alert sounded off.

"Bots, establish a field around the pod, but do not destroy organic matter!" Beth got the order out in time, and they followed her directions.

Through the bubble they formed, she saw a bed of white cloth and a long pile of dirt.

"Sissy, how is the body gone? Is this not a cryo-chamber?"

"Though the chamber appears to be intact, there are micro-cracks throughout the outer casing. It is probable that this individual suffocated and decayed naturally. The substance you see is organic matter, and my scans have picked up a faint life energy element."

"And radiation?"

"None present."

"Alrighty. Have the bots contain the life energy element, and let's collect some of the body for reanimation."

Beth felt elation at the thought; this was her best find ever. The field around the chamber turned red.

"There is a full DNA strand. Reanimation process will commence."

The sample got sucked away and added to the basic organic fluids needed to get started. First was the skeletal development. Two arms, one head, ten toes, and fingers. Next the organs started. Red, moist, and moving.

"Is it pure human?"

"Yes," Sissy said in her robotic voice.

The specimen finished. A female human shape lay in the metal growth compartment. The body was perfect. No excess body fat, only lean and muscled limbs. The skin was firm and pale. Better yet was the shiny, long hair, as dark as space itself. *Now time to reunite body and being.*

"Bots, remove all materials from the pod and store in a cryo-locker. Then place the body back into the pod. Our guest needs to settle into her skin if we expect conversation."

Beth swayed to the music. A female voice sang about living to see the seven wonders. On her counter was a book she'd found on a trip that described human food and how to cook it.

"Okay, I made the tomatoes hot. But I don't have any meat. Dang it, should have made a trip for some. Too late now. What if I smash the tomatoes and add some protein powder? There, it's like a soup! Smells good," Beth said to no one in particular.

The alarms from the medical bay went off.

"She's awake! Just in time for dinner." Beth shook her body, feeling her extra limbs morph into just two of everything.

She stepped into her jumper suit—or rather, that's what the plastic she'd found it in had called it. She zipped up and made her way through her living space to the medical area.

"Hello, please stay in the medical area. Beth will be with you momentarily," Beth heard Sissy say to their guest.

"Oh, Sissy, such good manners!" She stopped outside the sealed bay doors.

"Where am I?" The human female stood, looking around the sterilized room.

Beth had left a set of replicated human garments. The human had dressed; this pleased Beth. A funny cat with a taco stared at Beth from the human's shirt. She liked the space pattern behind the furry little thing.

"Sorry, I didn't want you to feel unprotected. Please, come on out. Sissy, open the bay doors." The sheets of glass parted.

Beth tilted her head. The human was so fragrant. Though most of the scent was foreign, Beth thought it reminded her of Earth itself. She decided she liked it, a lot.

"I'm Dr. Ronda Williams. Who are you?" She didn't leave the room. Beth noticed she leaned a little on the cryo-tube she'd been resting in.

"Oh, sorry, I'm Beth. I found your pod and brought you to my home. I've prepared some food. I thought you might feel hungry after your journey." She smiled, happy she'd remembered to make her teeth more human sized.

"I do feel…hungry."

"Well then, please follow me this way." Beth walked ahead, letting Dr. Ronda Williams follow her.

Beth's organs grumbled. She was starting to feel hunger herself. She took another lungful of the new scent, Dr. Ronda Williams. The song changed in the background. More classical music filled the air. Beth hummed the melodies. The doctor moved slowly with stiff steps but soon worked out most of the kinks.

They sat across from one another. Beth had put some of the food in a bowl but hadn't touched it, only drinking from her dark cylinder bottle.

"So, what do you remember?" Beth asked; she wanted as many details as she could get.

Beth's guest looked at her bowl of smashed soup and tried a little. She moved slowly, a side effect of reanimation.

"The world was overrun by the mutated strand of bacteria." She looked up at Beth, blinking a few times. "Sorry, the memories are a little fuzzy. The bacteria…it had killed all the food, and the water was slowly becoming undrinkable."

Beth coaxed her guest to eat more with an encouraging wave of her hand. She knew the protein would help the body wake up more.

After a moment, the doctor continued. "We had to abandon Earth. Those of us who had stayed behind, that is. But our ships had bombs on them. We barely escaped by shooting out the cryo-chambers. Did you hear our beacons?" Dr. Ronda Williams sat up, an alert look on her face now.

"How many pods got deployed?" Beth asked, ignoring the question as a curious need filled her tone. She leaned forward, eager to know the answer.

"Where did you say we were?" The doctor swallowed the food, making a face as if it weren't easy to do.

Beth knew all too well that replicated food was never the same as organic. A long pause passed between the two of them. Dr. Ronda Williams was starting to look more closely at Beth. Would she observe the differences between them? For example, Beth noticed the human blinked a lot, where she did not blink at all.

"Let me tell you what you've missed." Beth moved her chair closer to her guest. "The mutated bacteria you have spoken about became the next phase in human evolution. Since humans lived, these bacteria lived, too. So to threaten the life of one, you threatened the life of both. The two merged, creating a new, more-evolved species. There was no choice. Your kind had threatened its very existence."

"M4-61? Yes, I remember now. It started killing off every other kind of bacteria. It became airborne. We couldn't control it. People abused the formula, using it without thought to what it was doing to the environment." The doctor stared off blankly. "I recall the first reports of the spray getting into the environment. It had been tested in a controlled way. We never thought it could infest the wild. The organisms of the world had turned against the humans. The germaphobes almost succeeded in killing every germ until the organisms we needed turned against mankind. This is what you're talking about, right?"

"We had to stop it. We had the right to live, too. Sure some of my ancestors hurt the humans. But we helped you more. And we thought we had turned all those who'd been in the silver pods. I've seen the pictures in my history books. And now you're saying there are still pure humans out there? How exciting!"

"History books? What year is it?" The doctor didn't move, even as Beth's hand lightly touched hers.

"I believe it is close to what you would call the year thirty-five ten."

"What? That's over eight hundred years. Wait, we? Are you one of the bacterial evolutions?"

"Well, there are those in my family who would say I'm closer to the human chromosomes in my makeup. Obsessed with all things human, rebellious, and simply too damn independent." Beth smiled, letting her teeth look a little less square. Each became slightly pointed, but she couldn't help that now. "What they haven't realized is just how dangerous I've become."

"I feel light-headed." The doctor looked down, finally noticing something on her hand.

Beth's arm was there, but her hand had become some sort of purplish-black growth. It spread halfway up the doctor's arm.

"Please don't kill me," the doctor begged, sounding week and frail. Effects of the paralysis serum Beth had pumped into her blood.

"Oh, Dr. Ronda Williams, you will not be consumed fully. I can grow back the limb for you. I've just never had a taste of human. Although, technically, it's like cannibalism, I suppose." Beth spoke with a light and cheery voice.

The doctor's eyes bulged. Beth couldn't decide if she were relieved or terrified. *Probably both.* This was her greatest find by far.

"We are going to have quite an adventure together."

ABOUT THE COVER ARTIST

Verstandt R. A. Shelton is Inklings Publishing's cover artist. Growing up as a childhood misfit, Verstandt R. A. Shelton wiled away the hours daydreaming of floating in space and sitting at the bottom of the ocean floor. A disquieting obsession for the less beaten paths of philosophical ponderings and environmental extremes led him to stumble into the murky depths of the writerly craft. You can find him today chained in the back of his closet with the lights out, a bottle of whiskey in hand, and the ghosts of his inspirations (Stephen King, Clive Barker, Milton, Lovecraft, and Dante) breathing down his neck, writing stories to terrify the world. His lovely wife, Jennifer, and his cat, Siouxsie Q, worry for his safety.

ABOUT THE AUTHORS

Andrea Barbosa is the author of *Massive Black Hole*, *Olympian Passion*, and *Holes in Space*. She has a bachelor's degree in Tourism. She took creative writing courses at Texas Tech University. She loves to travel, read, and write poetry and fiction. She maintains an Indie review blog and was a contributor on Yahoo Contributor Network and Yahoo! Voices websites. Her work has been influenced by Joyce Carol Oates, Erica Jong, Sylvia Plath, and contemporary Brazilian authors Paulo Coelho and Fernando Sabino, among others. Currently, she serves as Author Events Director for the Houston Writers Guild.

Cathy Clay is a native Houstonian. She earned a bachelor's degree in Creative Writing from the University of Houston and a master's in English from Texas Southern University. *Agatta*, her debut novel, was published in 2010. Her scholarly reviews have been published in the *World Novel Compendium*, and her short stories and poems have been featured in literary journals, such as *Two Cities Review*. Another of her short stories appears in *Eclectically Criminal* by Inklings Publishing. In addition to writing, she enjoys family, animals, and the arts.

Mollie Anne Gates is an artist whose works have been hung in both group and individual shows in contemporary galleries. Her M.A. in Clinical Psychology influences her writing, as does her favorite pastime as a dreamer. Her early years spent curled up with her nose in a book in her aunt's bookstore led her to discover that books open doors into worlds where dreamers feel at home.

D. Marie Prokop was born in Pennsylvania. Her favorite fiction authors include Madeline L'Engle, Pearl S. Buck, and C.S. Lewis. In 2011, D. Marie participated in the National Novel Writing Month challenge and became enamored with fiction writing. NaNoWriMo helped D. Marie develop her young adult science fiction trilogy, Days of the Guardian. Its three volumes are *The Red String*, *The Red Cloak*, and *The Red Knot*. She has published a Christian fantasy short story for YA readers called "On The Outward Appearance" and also completed a short story for Middle Grade children entitled "The Baiji," a cultural and environmental tale involving friendship and loss. A singer-songwriter and avid knitter, D. Marie and her family now reside in Houston, Texas, along with three cats and much yarn.

Chantell Renee has written most of her life. Poetry, short stories, and now a YA series. Poetry continues to be her emotional outlet, with each line full of meaning, while her short stories range from horror to urban fantasy. Her debut series, The Shifter Series, focuses on supernatural creatures such as shape shifters and the Cruen, her twist on vampires. The first two books are available on Amazon, the third and final book will release January 13, 2017. She also has stories in the Inklings anthology *Eclectically Carnal* and the Skipjack Publishing anthology *Tides of Impossibility*. Spider Road Press published some of her poetry in their collection *In the Questions: Poetry by and about Strong Women*. And last, but not final, the upcoming *Hair Raising Tales of Horror* by Limitless Ink Pub will feature her stories. You can find all these titles on Amazon.com. You can keep up with this author at chantellrenee.com or chantell@chantellrenee1 on twitter, CRrenee_ on Instagram, chantellreneeblog.wordpress.com, Chantell renee/Limitlessinkauthor

Verstandt R. A. Shelton is Inklings Publishing's cover artist. Growing up as a childhood misfit, Verstandt R. A. Shelton wiled away the hours daydreaming of floating in space and sitting at the bottom of the ocean floor. A disquieting obsession for the less beaten paths of philosophical ponderings and environmental extremes led him to stumble into the murky depths of the writerly craft. You can find him today chained in the back of his closet with the lights out, a bottle of whiskey in hand, and the ghosts of his inspirations (Stephen King, Clive Barker, Milton, Lovecraft, and Dante) breathing down his neck, writing stories to terrify the world. His lovely wife, Jennifer, and his cat, Siouxsie Q, worry for his safety.

Thomas Edward Smith is an aspiring fantasy, sci-fi, and horror writer currently living in Perth, Western Australia. By day, he works as a second mate aboard commercial vessels on the West Australian coast. By night, he is secretly The Bluebird, a royalist superhero smiting the evil parliamentarians and their foul democratic process. Or did he just imagine that…Born in the United Kingdom, Thomas grew up on the Sunshine Coast in Queensland, Australia, before returning to the United Kingdom during his high school years. Upon graduating from Lancaster University, he moved back to Australia and has since spent no longer than a year in one place. He dreams of one day screwing everyone on the Earth and going home to Mars. Failing that, he'd like to retire to a duck farm and one day have a little girl with his eyes to spoil rotten.

Dorothy Tinker is a genre fiction writer, with a heavy focus on epic high fantasy. She is the author of the Peace of Evon young adult series, with three books published and the fourth book of the series in progress. She also has a growing collection of published short stories, including two fantasy/romance shorts in the Houston Writers Guild Press anthology, *Riding the Waves*, and a fantasy flash fiction piece in Writespace's *In Medias Res* anthology. Dorothy is an enthusiast of languages, cultures, and fantastical worlds.

Peter Venable has written both free and metric verse for over fifty years and been published in *Time of Singing, Windhover—A Journal of Christian Literature, The Whirlwind Review, Apex Magazine, The Christian Communicator,* and others. He is a semi-retired clinician, volunteers at a prison camp and food pantry, sings in the annual December Messiah, and is graced with a happy marriage, a wonderful daughter and son-in-law, and Yeshua.

Other Books by
Inklings Publishing &
Inklings Children Division

The Twisted Reveries series by Meg Hafdahl debuted in October 2015 with *Thirteen Tales of the Macabre*. In October 2016, *Tales from Willoughby* followed. Get your copy of these spine-tingling volumes today, and enjoy short stories by this great new female voice in horror!

Enjoy more short stories in the Eclectic Writings Series anthologies. Featuring a variety of great authors and each based on a theme, this collection will surprise and entertain. Get your copy of each of the four volumes in the series today!

This international legal thriller is the first book in the Roberto Duran series. Get to know this intrepid criminal attorney from Houston as he fights to uncover the truth and save a young Mexican socialite from wrongful incarceration.

This bilingual resource will provide insight into the workings of a civil lawsuit in terms anyone can understand. Great for interpreters, as well as authors who are writing legal thrillers.

Interpreters'
Anatomy *of a*
Civil Lawsuit

Anatomía *de un*
Juicio Civil *para*
Intérpretes Judiciales

Ramón M. del Villar

Attorney at Law
Federally Certified Court Interpreter
State Licensed Court Interpreter

Licenciado en Derecho
Intérprete Judicial Certificación Federal
Intérprete Judicial Texas, Maestría

The *Smiley Face Blatoon* launched Inklings Children Division in Summer 2015. Winner of the Texas Authors Association's First Place for Best Picture Book for all Ages, this, and all Inklings Children books, contains extension activities, discussion questions, and cross-curricular work, as well as other tools for parents and educators.

Perceptions Series
Volume One

Edited by: Fern Brady

The Perceptions Series anthologies are a collection of short stories, poems, and nonfiction articles based on themes written for children grades three through six by a variety of authors. As with all Inklings Children Division books, each volume contains questions and activities for parents and educators to extend learning.

Follow Inklings Publishing by:

 Signing up for our newsletter
on our website
www.inklingspublishing.com

 Liking our Facebook page

 Following our tweets

www.ingramcontent.com/pod-product-compliance
Lightning Source LLC
Chambersburg PA
CBHW051924220626
47052CB00003B/567